T0196126

PURGATORY'S BRIDGE

THE ONLY LINK TO ALL

Z. GARCIA

authorHOUSE®

AuthorHouse™
1663 Liberty Drive
Bloomington, IN 47403
www.authorhouse.com
Phone: 1 (800) 839-8640

Published by AuthorHouse 02/15/2017

ISBN: 978-1-5246-7189-1 (sc)
ISBN: 978-1-5246-7188-4 (e)

Print information available on the last page.

Any people depicted in stock imagery provided by Thinkstock are models,
and such images are being used for illustrative purposes only.
Certain stock imagery © Thinkstock.

This book is printed on acid-free paper.

Because of the dynamic nature of the Internet, any web addresses or
links contained in this book may have changed since publication and
may no longer be valid. The views expressed in this work are solely those
of the author and do not necessarily reflect the views of the publisher,
and the publisher hereby disclaims any responsibility for them.

CONTENTS

CONTENTS

PROLOGUE

I've figured out why people want to choose death over life sometimes. With all the circumstances we live with and the hell we pass through, you'd think that there'd be some kind of relief when it's all over. But what if you have unfinished business and it was an unexpected occurrence. The fact it's more complicated than that kinda sucks. Now you're left with some questions, right? My biggest question was what if you had a choice, to go back and finish your life or to start over on a whole new page. Sadly I can't resolve those issues either. So I guess that's why in my opinion people should say what's on their mind. Also because I really can't take hints very well ha-ha

CHAPTER 1

Ya'know, the funny thing about all of life's little surprises is that none of them seem to be so little. As the sunflower petals dance with the wind and the sky, a solemn promise was made. A memory lost by one but always remembered by another. "Takashi, promise me!", Said the cheerful little girl that was sitting across from me on what seems to be a plaid baby blue and white blanket with a raspberry pie in the middle of us. Two slices were cut out of the pie, one for me, and one for her. Putting two and two together, I realized that I was on a date with the girl. I also saw that I was no older than her at this moment. Although, something felt different. My chest wouldn't stop pounding; a heat started to cover my face as if a warm wet rag was placed over it. But at the same time, it feels distant........cold. Shadows began to engulf my surroundings as a tear streamed down the little girl's face. The only thing even scarier than that is that I'm looking

1

directly at her, but I can't paint a clear picture of what her face even looks like. "Promise me," Her words echoed in my head growing more and more frightening each time it is said. Just then a fire burst out of the ground covering my vision. With a final flash, I looked around thinking I was losing my mind only to find myself in my bed, in my room, in my apartment. Hi, I'm Takashi. Just in case, anyone missed it. "ahh..........nothing more than a dream", I sighed softly as I turned off my alarm which woke me. Honestly, I'm glad it did. I've been having similar dreams for a couple of days now; the ending changes every time, and it never gets better. So far, I just had the scariest one last night. Making my way towards the kitchen to make a bowl of cereal, the TV was broadcasting the news. "Schtttttsshh.......And in other news. A large number of natural disasters have been occurring recently leaving thousands of people homeless and hundreds missing. Many families have had to move halfway across the country due to the storms' damage...schttsh...", Well since I've just started to live by myself it's been a little difficult for me to fully live alone and go to college at the same time, but I manage. Believe it or not, college and high school are remarkably similar to each other.

Eating my Corn Flakes with chopped strawberries and bananas, I realize that I got to throw my breakfast out the window because I'm already 30 minutes late for class, "ahh dammit." I grab my book bag and proceed to haul ass down to the school; I don't get noticed much so being half an hour late shouldn't be a problem, right? "Crap, crap, crap, crap, crap, crap SHIT!!!!", I kept yelling at myself while running to school, trying to scold myself for being late. Then outta nowhere, just like my cereal this morning, my sense of balance just went flying out the window. I crashed into someone while telling myself to pay attention, huh, pretty ironic. "Oh I'm so sorry, you okay?", I said hesitantly trying to pick up everything that fell. Looking up to see who it was, I don't know if it was the best thing to happen to me or the worst, but at that moment.....I didn't even want to go to school anymore. She had a very light lavender hair that seemed almost white if you were to see it under the moonlight reaching down to the middle of her back. Her eyes shined a bright royal purple glow, like a crystal encrusted in a pearl. When she smiled and spoke...well, I guess you could say that was it. "No worries man," She said not looking concerned at all about me crashing into her, but she seemed to be in a huge hurry. I gave her the bag. Before I could say anything. "Okay thanks, man, gotta go bye!".She dropped a wooden box out o her bag. At first, it looked like a traditional jewelry box, carvings and all. "Wait! You forgot-", I tried calling out to her, but she was already gone, so fast. She left the box behind. Looking at it more it looked....different. It looked older; ancient is how I should put it, the carvings were something greek or roman, yet had some small crests on the corners showing satanic and angelic symbols, what kinda' is this? Hey, wait. I got lost questioning myself"Where am I?",

"Not in class that's where" a familiar voice spoke out. Gruff, but friendly. It was my classmate Arashi. He's the popular guy in college, pretty much everything you'd expect from one too. The tall, athletic type. Smooth with school, and with girls, he's the complete opposite of me in school, and for some reason, unlike most people, He didn't ignore me or was mean to me, he actually wanted to be my friend."I'm already here?", I said completely dumbfounded. I don't even remember getting here. "You're skipping 1st. Period too huh? Rare. So, who is she? ", He said chuckling. Honestly, I was confused. "what are you talking about?", I asked. "Don't play dumb. I'm practically your only friend here, no offense. Plus, you may be late all the time, but you never skip class". Wait, you don't mean? I just ran into her. "I just overslept that's all," The fuck? Am I trying to lie, I-I'm really trying to hide her from my friend, but why? "Well anyway man, I gotta tell you somethin' check it out, remember the tornado that happened in town last week?". He's referring to all the random natural disasters that have been happening lately on the news. A tornado hit my town but luckily, it only hit half of my city. "Yea I remember," I said recollecting on it for a bit. "Well there was a museum on that side of the city, and it was also hit, they recovered many items, but they're still looking for the rest of the artifacts, even a bunch of collectors showed up trying to find the items before the museum does" He's a huge fan of historical figures and all that has to do with them. He then goes on by pulling out a newspaper from this morning. It had a list of the items and the pictures next to them. Damn!! the rewards here are friggin crazy!! 10,000 dollars for a ring....wait. The encryption on it looks like the box that the girl left behind, the same box that in my backpack. "Arashi, Why do you have this?" looking up back at him I can already see money in his eyes and a light bulb on his head. he's planning to look for them and wants me to help him. "No, we are not doin' this again," I told him. The last time I helped you make money, I had to keep watch while you took pictures of the girls changing in the locker room," It wasn't his first cash scheme either. "and besides I heard like a lot of people have been going missing lately. Screw that," Arashi replied eagerly: "Man that just because people got lost in the storms. Besides it's not gonna be like last time, this time, we can make money and not catch any heat for it." He said trying to ensure me. Because the last time we got caught, the both of us had to clean the boy's bathrooms for a week, ALL of them. "ahh...alright but wait til after class, please? I didn't try to miss the 1st class, and I'm not trying to miss the rest of today." I told him. "Awesome," He said excitedly. "I'll come back when class is over so we can go,". "okay but what are you gonna do til then?", I asked him, He smiled and simply replied "dunno, See ya," that answer concerned me a bit, but my morning was already trippy a hell, and I just wanted to chill out at this point, so I just went to class.

Pretty much the whole day went by the same as any other, but one thing still kept getting to me, the encryption on the ring in the newspaper. I swear it's the same one from that box in my backpack. I haven't had time to make sure due to my classes, but I'm going to. And honestly, it smells. I also started to think about my dreams; they were all pretty much the same except the ending changed every time. The first one ended with a grim reaper just standing there; then he reached ou his hand, and it felt like everything that made me was separating from me, and I felt powerless, it just only got worse with the constant shift in endings. Then I started to think about that girl again. There are a lot of cute girls in this school, and I've even thought about asking out one of them too. She was prettier than every single one of them. I wish I could see her again. That smile that looked so gentle yet fierce. Her hair looking like someone managed

5

to get one of the best pearls in the world and cut them into beautiful locks just for her, I could see her now, standing at the door of the classroom waving at me. Wait..........I-I can see her, SHE'S HERE!!! "Takashi," my teacher called me knocking me out of my state of shock. "Yess!" I replied without missing a beat because I don't know if I'm even seeing the right thing right now. That girl from earlier, that same girl, she's standing next to my teacher, she's literally right there, she knows I have the box. "Your girlfriend is here to take you to your doctor's appointment. Why didn't you let me know you were going to the doctor today, your health is important", My teacher said completely oblivious to my dumbfounded face because honestly, I have no clue what the FUCK SHE'S TALKING ABOUT!!! As I'm walking to the front of the room, the girl spoke, "Cmon Babe, we still gotta go to your place first," I never thought I'd be seeing that smile ever again, I-its getting closer. This sensation, so soft, warm. She's kissing me, she took my first kiss. I don't even know who she is, but she's kissing me like this. "We're gonna be late" While we took off, she grabbed my hand. Ya'know, despite knowing the real reason why she's here. Frankly, I'm not that disappointed. In the midst of this happy moment, I can hear the other students whispering amongst each other asking who was she and how is she, my girlfriend. I wouldn't blame them really, besides Kenshiro, I didn't really have any friends at school, Wait, How are we back at my apartment? Aarrghh, I spaced out again. She brought me to my apartment and shut all the blinds and started to peek outside as if she's hiding from someone but what for? "Cool, the law won't find me here," she said in a sigh of relief. someone WAS looking for her. "Hey man, I am soo sorry about what happened today I really didn't mean to cause all that- Oh! My bad. Hi, I'm Yosuna Hatake," She shook my hand, "And you are?". At first, I was caught up in just looking at her, the only thing on my mind was that she's holding my hand "I'm Takashi...Takashi Azuno "Then a thought hit me so hard that I couldn't help but just to blurt it out. "Wait, how'd you know where to find me? WHAT THE HELL IS GOING ON, WHY ARE YOU RUNNING FROM THE COPS?!?." I don't know exactly what her reaction would be but without missing a beat she replied "See, That's what I'm apologizing for", This girl had completely lost her mind "Look, I can explain everything that's going on but first, I dropped something when I bumped into you this morning, and it's kind of a big deal to me. You don't happen to have nd old wooden box with you do ya?" I knew it, to be honest, I'm getting kinda curious about it now. No!! I better not get caught up in this mess, I already got a lot on my plate, I better just give it back. Grabbing the box, I replied "Yea. It's over here, hey uhh it smells kinda funny for some-AH" I tripped, no, something tripped me. I fell straight to the ground dropping the box as well. "NO!!" We both blurted out at the same time as the box fell on its corner and cracked wide open."I'm so sorry I-", Outcome a big stockpile of weed with two ancient medallions.Rendered speechless, I had no clue what to think at this moment, but all I knew was I wanted no part of this shit. I start scooping all the weed back into the box without saying a word, literally freaking out inside my mind," my bad man, look lemme get this, and I'll be outta ya hair," Yosuna said helping me clean but just as freaked out. Almost done cleaning everything I grab the medallion and she yells out "WAIT, don't touch it!", But I already had it in my hand, "Oh Shit," A slight boom exploded from, both medallions with a blinding light shining off of them. The aura from the It was at this moment that I knew, I fucked up.

CHAPTER 2

As the lights grew brighter and brighter, everything started to shake. With every rumble, I can feel my heart gradually sinking down past my feet. I'm losing it at this point and Yosuna's looks.....scared as if what I did was the most horrible thing a human being was capable of. Out of instinct, I grabbed her to make sure she wouldn't get hurt. As I'm holding her, I saw something familiar, a flame, the same burst of fire from the dream I had this morning. Just what the hell is going on? The light was expanding rapidly, but then, everything reverted. Everything went back to normal, Well except for the fact that there are TWO NEW STRANGERS in my apartment. Two guys, they look about thirtyish with a very unpleasant aura coming off both of them. The one one the right looked slick, Long red hair in what seems to be a red and black suit with the design having a burned and ripped edges on the collars. The one on the left didn't look so flashy. He actually resembled an ordinary businessman. Glasses, short rugged hair, suit and all. Although Something was off, his ears, it was pointed. Not that of an elf but that of a creature, more along the line of an oni. No, a demon. He also seemed to have a certain charm that almost seems a bit too trustworthy. The thing about them is that they both happen to have the same kind of presence. A dark and evil presence that did way more than just scare the shit out of me. I was starting to have a mental breakdown due to pure fear. I just saw the regular life that I wanted to start on my own start fading into the darkness brought on by these two. I began to understand what Yosuna was feeling now. The man with the glasses spoke, "Ahh Whats going on here, Where am I?" Then the other man as well, "ugh..I'm gonna kill the son of a bitch who did this to me!!" Yea, I don't feel much better at all. They both noticed each other and said: "you did this!!, Huh?" They seemed confused for a second, I have no idea what possessed me to, but I took that second to ask: "Wait, who the hell are you?" Without missing a beat, the looked at me and replied: "I'm the ruler of Hell." They overheard their responses then stared at each other with a high disdain for what the other one had just said. "LIKE HELL YOU ARE!!" Then I heard everything that explained it all, who they were, how they got here, the scary ass aura. I feel now that I would've been better not knowing at all.

The long haired man started off: "How dare you ask who I am. I am Hades!!. Son of the Titan Cronus and Rhea. God of the underworld and," Another voice interrupted. "Now let me stop you right there you walking delusion of an idiot" The man in the glasses spoke so smoothly with no hesitation, it was almost slick. "First off, I created Hell, and as far as I'm concerned, I still run the place. Unmatched and unchallenged." They give each other an evil gaze that would send even the toughest guys running home. "And you are?" Hades asked sarcastically "Why I'm the morning star himself, not that it matters anyway." The morning star? "Lucifer," Yosuna said looking even more frightened. He continued to speak "For some knights of the round table punk like you to even call yourself a god is kinda......irritating" the atmosphere started to get darker. "You tend to threaten me Goggles!!. You have no idea just what kind of power I possess." Hades said completely offended and outraged by what Lucifer "Hmph! Talking about you created hell, give me a break-," A sudden blast of dark matter or energy resembling black and blue flames interrupted Hades throwing him through my restroom wall. "Goggles huh? Looks like somebody forgot how to use their manners" Lucifer said, his tone never changed, but you can tell he was angrily excited. What the Hell!!! What's going on?!? His aura is made of the same flame that blasted Hades, but it started to change form. His shadow took the shape of a beast with massive angel wings but demon horns. The apartment was starting to crumble little by little. With every rumbling step, he took walking towards Hades stretching out his hand to kill Hades he said: "My my...and you're a so called God, don't get ahead of yourself," Lucifer was hit with a counter-blast from Hades sent him flying out my window and crashed into the street. At the look of it, it was similar to Lucifer's power, dark matter or energy resembling black and blue flames. But the color of Hades' power was red. His shadow and aura made the same transformation except it was all out a demon, the wings as well. I want to leave, run out this building as fast as humanly fucking possible......but......but, my feet.....won't move. I'm stuck at a stand still between my will to leave and my nerve to run. Frozen inside my own head, Yosuna brought me back to reality when grabbed me: "HEYY!! We gotta go now!!" I followed her running out the apartment, my mind still trying to take in all of what just happened. Like right now, everyone is leaving the building as its beginning to look like the other side of the city. Hades levitates out of the apartment window down in front of the huge crater where Lucifer obviously crashed into the street. "you're strong, I'm gonna enjoy killing you.", Lucifer stood up wiping himself off as he replied; "Please, how can you kill someone who's already DEAD!!!" Dark gray clouds covered the sky, along followed thunder and rain. Another storm was coming.

Lucifer dashes towards Hades and the fight begins, he throws two kicks that were blocked followed up with A three-hit combo which partially connected. Hades counters with a right cross which such power that the wind effect alone from the attack sliced nearby...everything, that's not human at all!! they continue to exchange blows so frequently it was as if they looked like live wrecking ball breaking down anything they ran into. This was getting way outta control way too fast, I needed to stop them. I jetted towards them, then in almost, before I could see it, Yosuna stepped in front of me, stopping me. "What the hell are you doing!?!?" I yelled at her completely baffled by the whole thing. "Dude, do you have no clue what the FUCK you did?!? She responded without missing a beat. She was right, just by name, who doesn't know these two are? Lucifer and Hades. It's a fight between the Devil and the Ruler of the underworld who is practically the same person in his own right. It was then when I saw it when I realized how big I actually screwed up. The fight raged on with not even a sign of them letting up until Lucifer hit Hades with a hard right knee to the gut which followed it with a left punch, launching Hades into the air. Then, within a blink of an eye, Lucifer lunged with a straight right kick connecting like a spear piercing a wild boar. Drilling kick after kick rotating and alternating right, left, right, left, spinning around the other side and finalizing with a solid blow with a fist surrounded by his flame and crashed Hades into a crater twice the size of the one he made when he hit. As Lucifer lands about 100 yards from the hole, Hades rises up from the rubble, laughing hysterically evil as they stare each other down, both covered in scrapes and scars. "I haven't had this much fun in ages. Let us kick it up a notch." The moment that was said, Hades released an evil growl that, not only can be heard for miles but sent the worst cold shiver down your spine that would bring out the bitch in any badass you can think of. The more I watched, the more I saw what it's like to mix your worst nightmare with your greatest fear.

The transformation was not pleasant to the eye. The earth quaked more and more, sinking deeper where he stood. Cars were flattened by the whiplash. He began to look like less of a man and more like the devil. Horns pierced through the skin on his forehead, the rest of it seemed to just boil to the point of looking burned to the crisp with red flames seeping through the cracks. His body grew in almost an instant. In 2 seconds just like that, he doubled in size, had claws for hands, and had large demon wings span the length of a school bus. I couldn't help but to blurt out: "WHAT THE FUCK IS THAT!?!? I'm losing my complete grasp on reality, and Lucifer barely seems impressed. "Hmph, this might have just gotten a bit more interesting," he said, pushing up his glasses and rolling up his sleeves. "Interesting huh?" Hades replied with a demonic chuckle" No, hehe, it's over." and before anyone could blink, he dashed behind Lucifer, almost looking like a teleport. Even Lucifer didn't expect that. "What!?!" He was hit with a hard backhanded right from Hades, sending him flying far. He then dashed to the other side, uppercutting Lucifer in the air, then continued to knock him around, bouncing him back and forth in the air with punches. Trying to finalize, Hades grabs Lucifer by the neck, and from over 250 feet in the air, slams him into the ground, breaking the pavement while dragging him. He then started punching, one after another, harder and harder with each punch. "Don't tell me this is all you have, I've only just begun!!" Hades yells with laughter. Then, the punches stop, but not by Hade's account. Another demonic-looking hand was grabbing hold of Hade's arm followed by an, even more, darker and angrier tone than his. "I'VE HAD ENOUGH OF THIS STUPIDITY!!!" The tables turned dramatically.

Hades was slammed into the pavement and thrown upwards. Lucifer wasn't gonna have his bullshit. He let out a roar that shook the spines of literally anything. Cars are now flying into buildings. The ground shook and sank twice as hard with every second he turned. But the way he changed was, different. It didn't look as unpleasant as Hade's, but it wasn't good either. For instance, Lucifer's skin didn't boil. His skin cracked with blue flames seeping through. It peeled off almost like flakes, with the outcome still a demonic beast. But his wings were that of an angel, although black that seemed to fade white at the very tip of the feathers. Hades teleports near Lucifer again, but one is not fooled twice."Not this time," With his left hand, Lucifer catches Hades by the neck, punches, backhands, the follows with a solid headbutt sounding like two semis's colliding shooting Hades into the ground. Hade's skips along the street like a tumbleweed before Lucifer catches him connecting with an uppercut. Hades eventually catches the drift and starts being serious. He blocked Lucifer's next upcoming attacks and counters with a couple of his own. It's a barrage of punches and kicks going back, and forth between the two demon lords. They rise up fighting continuously with auras now looking like massive purple fireworks going off in the sky with every explosion sending back a horrible whiplash. Then they separate. Hades laughs evilly. "How wonderful? You might actually be more fun than my brothers. But it's time to end this. The underworld is mine, and I will not allow filth like you to claim RULE!!!!!" Lucifer Solemnly replies in the same demonic tone from earlier. "Good. Because you're starting to become a real pain in my ass!" And with one charge they intend to end it. I don't know what the fuck I'm watching anymore. I see Yosuna frightened, but alert. "At this rate, they'll destroy the city" Eh, ARE YOU SHITTING ME RIGHT NOW!?!? I finally get a grip on myself and look around. This is real. My street is in shambles, people might have died, and it's my fault. I gotta fix it

CHAPTER 3

Ugh. The shit I do for people right? Alright. In the case of any confusion, here's what's going on from my point of view. My Dumbass accidentally released two of the most powerful and evil beings known to the Bible and Greek mythology. With the two having egos as huge as their reputations, tension escalated quickly. It then broke into a fight that nearly ran my street to rubble, and they're still at it. So now I'm trying to see how am I gonna stop all this crazy shit before it gets anymore insane than it already has. I did the first thing that came to mind, I ran towards the fight. "Takashi- eh-HEY!! Come back here! You're gonna get yourself killed!" Yosuna yelled at me, but I didn't listen. I grabbed a plumbing pipe from the floor and chucked it as far as I could at them. They glanced at it, and the damn thing shot back as if they blocked it just by looking at it. "Well, that ain't gonna work," I told myself trying to see what plan B was. I saw the two break apart and just stand across from each other covered in rubble and scars. Hades creates a sudden flame that summoned a 2-pronged fork. "That's it!! Time to end you!!" Yelled Hades. Lucifer just calmly replied, "Just die already!" as Hades and Lucifer charged simultaneously. I did the only thing stupid enough to either make a difference, or make jack shit, but I'm gonna die anyway so, what's the point? I ran in between them. The last thing I heard was Yosuna scream "TAKASHI!!!"

Black. That's all I can see. I'm moving my hands in front of my own face, walking around to find anything, nothing. The last thing I remember seeing was blood, my blood......I was...stabbed. My heart was pounding harder than a drum. I was shaking, not only because it felt arctic cold, but I was so scared, that was all my nerves could do. "HELLO!?!" I called out seeing if anyone, just anyone, could hear me. Don't tell me, I'm...I'm dead. No, please, PLEASE!?! Then, a split second before I was gonna crack, a great white spark flashed, and I woke up somewhere in the middle of some gray woods, at the end of it, my childhood home. It was all here. The long driveway, the swing near the lake with the dock where the cherry blossom petals floated on in the fall. There it was, my house, all here. "What- what is this?" I asked too overwhelmed by the scenery. "You don't recognize it? This is where you grew up." Someone answered me. Wait, I know that voice...it can't be. I couldn't help it. Butterflies were in my stomach, my eyes watered. I turned around, the only way to make sure, right? A woman stood behind me in perfect posture. Her lively brown hair was held in a single ponytail. She was wearing a thin brownish-white sweater with a soft pink apron and the most gentle smile that would make a psycho turn sane. It was her, the only woman I haven't seen since I was 4. I trembled when I spoke "M-Mom?"

"Hello, Takashi, My how you've grown?" She replied. Her soft-spoken voice was just the same as I remember it. That settles it, I'm dead. But at this moment, I couldn't care less. In all emotion and instinct, I immediately ran and hugged her. "Mom!" I said sobbing in her arms as if I was a kid again. "I missed you, I missed you so much!" I repeated to her making sure she heard it. "It's been so long since that day, oh how I've missed so," She said to me and she didn't have to say it twice. I had so many questions to ask, but before I said anything she spoke first. "Listen, there is not much time," "Wait, I need more time," I replied wanting to ask at least one question. "Please listen," She said stopping me, so I listened. "You're not supposed to be here. There is still so much for you to do. Find your father, he is still out there, he'll help you. I have faith we'll meet again." Her words were reassuring, I don't know why but they were. "Wait!! What do you mean? Wait! MOM!!" I got sidetracked as I called out to her but she was already gone. Then I heard her say one more thing. "When the two paths show, go left." After she had said that, the street behind her split into two roads. As I said before, her words were reassuring, I don't know why but they were. So I took the road on the left. I ran as hard as I could to see if it'll at least takes me somewhere. It took me to this soft feeling light, then I woke up.

I'm in my room, it's morning, was it? I guess it was, a dream, but it felt so real. Well, at least everything seems back to normal. I turn over to rest a little bit more before I get up, I can't. There's extra weight on one side of my body.

Is someone else sleeping with me? I pick up my blanket to check. A girl was also sleeping in my bed, It's Yosuna. Funny thing is she looks cuter when she's asleep, maybe even peaceful. I remembered the kiss, so passionate, soft as if she knew me already. Then I noticed something else. I couldn't help it, I yelled: "WHAT THE HELL IS GOIN ON!?!? WHY ARE YOU NAKED!?!?," She was. She woke up and saw my baffled expression. "You're awake!!!" In the drop of a hat, she hugged me. "Oh thank God," her grip tightened. It was nice, but it didn't answer my question. "Wait, yesterday was real? Hades, Lucifer,?" I asked her. Maybe I should've asked that first. "They're gone, so we're safe, there's a lot to explain exactly what kinda mess you got yourself into," She replied. "But first.". After that small quiet moment of her holding me, she let go, and in a snap, slapped me and started to chew me out. Honestly, she is blatantly rude. "What the hell were you thinking!? If I weren't there to heal you, you would've died,". "Healed me?" I asked her seeing if I heard correctly. "do you see any scars," She said answering a question with a question. I didn't realize it, but she's right. I checked under my shirt, it looks like yesterday never happened. "so what, you fixed my apartment, and the street too huh? Do you have powers or somethin'?" I asked sarcastically. She didn't say anything. "it was a joke," I said, but her face didn't change, in fact, she nodded in response. "Yea, actually. Well, not the street, just your apartment." I checked out the window, The Street is wrecked. She then grabbed the knife from the kitchen reached out and gave herself a very nasty slit in her right arm. "Wha-what the HELL ARE YOU DOING!?! I yelled, completely thrown off. She covered the cut with her other arm. After a second a greenish-lavender light glowed from where she held. Let go, and there was nothing there. Yosuna was telling the truth. She grabbed my hands "Like I said, there's a lot to explain. So can you please hear me out?", I know it sounds strange but, it's almost as if I can feel her honesty while she's holding my hands. Ok, so yesterday was real. She did get me home, ahh I might as well listen. "Okay I will, but first, can you put some clothes on first?" I said trying to look away because all she did was put on one of my shirts, not as easy thing to do. "Yo Takashi, ya home? I got breakfast" someone came into the room. There's only one other person who has the key to my apartment, my landlord. In an instant, he backed away then shut the door, and now there's an awkward silence.

CHAPTER 4

It's no mistake what it looked like, I brought a girl home last night, we're still in my bed, and all she has on is my t-shirt. If only. "Hey Kenshi, hehe ahh how ya doin'?" I said, breaking the ice as Yosuna and I get dressed and walk into the living room. The radio was playing lighter shade of brown. The whole apartment smelled like the breakfast Kenshi had cooking in the kitchen. Pancakes with egg omelet and bacon "Not as good as you are apparently. I didn't know someone stayed over last night, I really didn't mean to interrupt anything," He said proudly laughing off the situation. He's not like typical landlords. Kenshi seems just like a regular guy actually. You wouldn't even guess he owned the building. "Yo Takashi, who's the random guy who just let himself in?" Yosuna asked me, paranoid about him. "That's Kenshi, He's my landlord, slash, caretaker," I replied honestly as I walked to the table. "Caretaker? What,

21

are you adopted or something?" She asked me. "uh, yeah, actually," I answered, I don't like thinking about it that much. "Oh, uh forget I said anything," Yosuna told me, I guess she knew. "Nah it's okay. It'll explain Kenshi too," I said, why not right? I told her everything "When I was 4 years old, my parents and I were on vacation to Mt. Fuji. We had an accident on the way there. I was the only one they found. After a while, they still couldn't find my mom and dad, so I was placed in a home for orphans and was adopted by Kenshi sometime later." She apologized for what happened, but I assured her that I was fine and over it already. Ya'know, even though I don't like thinking about this, it felt nice to talk to someone about it. And besides, I kinda liked having a cute girl around the place.

"Well, breakfast is ready," said Kenshi as he came into the dining room serving plates. "Takashi was 5 when I brought him home. Hahaha, he was so shy but I managed to get him to warm up to me and by the time you know it I was sending him to school. So what, you're not going to introduce me to your girlfriend" He nudges me a bit. "Oh yeah, wait, hey!" I replied as I introduced them to each other, and we begin to eat. After a very short pause, Kenshi asked us. "So how did you two meet?" he smiled as he asked. I kind of stuttered, due to the fact I didn't know how to answer that question. "I'm sorta new to town," Yosuna replied. "I didn't really have a place to stay the night. So, Takashi offered me to sleep here," She knows how to think quick, that's for sure. This was new to me as it was to him "Really? Smooth move casanova," Kenshi replied as he gave me a sly smile. "Way to go buddy!!" was what he was actually thinking. I have never dated any girls, so, me having one stay overnight was a first for me. After we had finished breakfast, Kenshi went home, and I just started getting ready for school. "So that's your story huh?" She asked me, more relaxed about everything now. "Yeah, that pretty much sums me up, What about you?" I responded I'm honestly curious now that I brought it up. She glanced at me smirked into a smile, sighed and said "Yeah, now that the other guy left, I can let you know what's going on. And I guess I'll tell you a little bit about myself too."

"Alright. You see, not only was yesterday real, you managed to get yourself stuck smack dead in the middle of it," Yosuna started off bluntly as always. I'd wish she sugarcoat it at least a bit. The only other thing that bugged me was, this was not getting any less bizarre. It appears that ancient deities and spiritual being from every religion and mythology exist, Like ALL of them. I listened as she went on. "A long time, about 900 years ago during the Crusades. A group of soldiers from the knight's templar discovered a deep cave underground and used it for shelter one night. It turns out they wandered into and camped at the gateway link to all the other realms. A place where the living should never go. Purgatory, which is where you were yesterday." Yesterday? Mom. Yosuna was as stern as ever while giving me the details: "You see this world is one of 200 realms that are connected through purgatory. The knights wound up not only releasing Lucifer and Hades but every demon-lord within mythology, religion, and folklore. They also opened the gate for every realm to connect. Lucifer and Hades never met in the last war due to Hades trying to take Olympus, while Lucifer went after Heaven. Even so, it was as still brutal. Imagine, every apocalypse from every belief setting off all at once. Why do you think the war took almost 200 years? To seal them back and restore everything to the way it was, and you just started it all over again" It didn't make sense. The reason for the crusades was for religious politics and during that time who knows what could've gone down, and I still can't explain how Yosuna healed herself in the first place. This sounds nuts. "Okay, So if it's all true, what do I get to do with this?" I asked because it looks to me it like it's blown over. Without missing a beat, she responded: "The one who releases the demon-lords is the only one who can seal them back, kinda cliche but, I don't make the rules. So until we find out how to fix this crap, I'm gonna stay here to keep an eye on you" Aand she's staying here too. That's obvious enough. Getting caught up in conversation, I saw that I was late to school, again. "Aww, Damn it. Hey, I gotta go, Just stay here until I come back, see ya," I said cutting our chat short. I grabbed what I needed and walked out the door.

Halfway to school, "DUDE!!" Someone called out to me, "What the hell man? I waited for you forever" It was Arashi, Oh shit I forgot about yesterday!! "Dude, I am so sorry. a lot happened yesterday" I told him trying to apologize for not meeting up with him. "It's cool man, hey guess what? I found some stuff!" He said excitedly not even caring about what I did. He grabbed his backpack and pulled out a ring with an Islamic imprint on the surface. "It's one of the rings from the flyer," He said explaining: Its name is the Seal of Solomon. It's made of Brass and iron but worth 25 thousand dollars." I could see why. I wanted to chat with him more on this, but I didn't have any more time. I was late as is. I cut him off saying I had to go to class, it was reasonable enough, so he just walked off saying: "Alright, see ya. I'm gonna go return this for the reward," I still don't get how he's able to be so famous in school and yet, go off on random adventures like this. During class, I couldn't help but think about everything that happened since yesterday. The box, the Devils fighting, the chaos. Just what the hell DID I get myself into? A bigger question, what does Yosuna have to do with any of this? *knock knock knock* Someone was at the classroom door. It was the Class President Mae. She was practically in the same league as Arashi. She was beautiful compared to the other college girls. Except for one thing, that she hardly ever spoke to me at all. She walked up right to my desk. "Hey you're Arashi's friend aren't you?" She asked me, it seems Mae and Arashi are both leaders of their athletic clubs. "Uh, Yeah" I answered a bit confused. "Would you mind following me to the roof for lunch please?" She asked me calmly with a sweet smile. Even though I knew, something was up. I accepted her invite.

CHAPTER 5

It was lunch when I ran into Mae, and I followed her to the roof. I was getting nervous. I started to sweat. Nothing like this ever happens to me. A girl walking up to me and asking me to come meet her to have lunch together. I mean, I did have a little crush on Mae once in the past, but that was hardly anything. We got to the roof of the school, and I asked her out of complete curiosity. "Mae, Thank you for inviting me to lunch, but why me? you hardly ever spoke to me in the past" I said wondering why now of all people who she could invite with no trouble at all, why me? "Because I'm interested in you," She murmured softly in response to my question. I was shocked "wait, huh? I asked to make sure. She turned around and shoved me against the wall. Gotten closer and whispered in my ear "I've been watching you for a while, Takashi. There's a thing about you that's... different from other guys." Her voice was sweet, soft, and seductive enough to give you goosebumps. This was going a bit too fast. I tried stalling: "Different hehe how? I don't see anything different, yup same ole me." I was babbling on, then she put both her hands on my face and whispered slowly: "Don't talk, Just kiss me." I couldn't help, it at this point I see why all the guys, even Arashi, wanted to try dating her. My eyes closed, our faces are drawn in, and at that moment her lips touched mine, I felt every goosebump fade away. Her lips were soft and warm, It was almost pure bliss. Hold on. Something doesn't feel right. My body's getting weak, It's like the longer I kiss her, the harder it is to move my own body. Her grip was getting stronger, then, she bit my neck "AAHH!!" I yelled out pain. A very light of blood started to flow. grr...Damn, I knew it, I walked into a trap.

I can feel my body getting colder, but my neck is burning like a fever. I was moving less and less the more I try to struggle out of Mae's grip. She was something else, nothing human I know that for sure. My mind was going blank, I was losing blood, I was using any bit of strength I had into getting her off of me. I didn't like this. Being taken advantage of like an idiot. It pissed me off. My blood boiled, and my eyes started to burn. My body twitched, then I felt an incredible amount of strength come back to me in an instant. "Get the hell...OFF OF ME!!" I yelled out, throwing her about 10 feet away from me. My legs gave out. Grabbing my neck, I dropped, trying to recover. Then, I felt something. There were only two teeth marks where she bit me. "What is this, what are you?" was the only thing I could ask. "isn't it obvious, I'm a vampire" She replied while she actually licked the blood off of her hand. after she said that, I saw it. Her fangs, They were pearly white and looked needle sharp. Her eyes glowed red-brown. She continued saying: "My my, I guess they weren't just rumors. You have their essence as well, I can taste it." "What, essence?" I said, getting up slowly. She started walking towards me. "Think back to what you did yesterday, Who you let out." She said, For some reason, I just knew it had something to do with yesterday. "You see, now you have something that everybody's gonna want, but I'm gonna get it first." She shoved me into the wall for the second time and proceeded to bite me again until someone grabbed her shoulder. "Let him go." Said another voice. A figure behind Mae stopping her from making a meal out of me. I recognized who it was and it turns out I wasn't the only one who knew.

"Yosuna Hatake, ain't this something? What are you, this boy's watchdog now?" Mae Said not letting up on her grip. "That's none of your business, Now let him go before I give you a heart murmur that opens your whole chest," Yosuna replied holding what looks to be a silver steak. Mae started to let go and back up. "Alright, how'd you get here?" Yosuna asked. Well, I guess they're not strangers huh? "I followed your scent genius, the rest was easy. You know as well as I do who he is now, what he is," Mae replied. "Besides, you could've stopped this, you've killed countless times to prevent messes like these. This can end now, two birds with one stone. How's this human any different?" "And you know as well as I do that this is much bigger than that." Yosuna sternly told her. "But getting you out the way might not do any harm, huh?" then nudges the steak, poking Mae's back. She was actually willing to do it, She was actually willing to kill my classmate. I mean, yeah this situation is out of whack, and I still don't know what the hell's going on, but I don't want anyone to die. "Yosuna, stop it," I said, hoping she won't take it any further. Yosuna wasn't paying attention to me she was still fixated on Mae, telling her: "You know, maybe I should flip a coin. Yea, heads, you live, tails." "YOSUNA STOP IT!!" I shouted. She was going too far. "Let her go. right now!" I told her "Why? She just tried to kill you," Yosuna replied. "NOW!" I said. "Alright, fine," Yosuna responded, releasing Mae. Mae looked at me. I could tell she was relieved to be released but confused that I let her go "Why?" she asked "I really don't think so," I replied. I could see from the start there was the same feeling I felt when Yosuna grabbed my hands. There's an absolute honesty in her heart that somehow shows me someone's real intention. It's weird but reassuring. "I can see it in your eyes," I told her. She stopped looking at me and just took off "Lunch is over, we gotta go to class," Mae said before hitting the door

"If you don't mind me asking. why did you let her go?" Yosuna asked, walking up to me lighting a cigarette. "I don't think she was really going to kill me," I answered. "and the next time we see her, hell, she might even help us" I went on. "Well, better hope you don't regret it, wanna drag?" She said offering the cigarette, wait, it smells funny. "Is that weed?" I asked, "Yeah, it is. Wanna?" she said casually. of course, it is "I'm good," I replied. The rest of the day went like nothing happened. I even passed by Mae in the hallway, nothing. I got home and washed up hoping to have some time to relax, but Yosuna was on the couch with 4 boxes of pizza. "Takashi, I gotta talk to you," she said, grabbing another slice. How many has she eaten? "Aww, come on. hasn't it been enough for one day?" I asked. "Are you kidding me? You almost died 2 days in a row, and it's not gonna get better. So you need to listen." I sighed and just sat on the couch and started eating. She went on telling me: "They didn't know about one another last time, but now that's changed. If anything, their conflict alone declared war on each other. Not only that, It wasn't even a single day and you were attacked. Talk about word spreading faster than wildfire. That means we have to start tomorrow, tonight we rest." "Huh," I said. "I have morning classes tomorrow." I still wasn't expecting something that wild. Yosuna pulled out some books based on religion and mythology and replied: "Fine when you're done with your damn classes, jeez. But we got to find a way to seal both of these guys back or pretty much everything's screwed. According to documents of the old world, or in your case the Bible's old testament, There was a ring, It's a seal actually, It is the seal of Solomon. There were 44 seals to be exact and each of them embedded in a ring, with an individual charm or power to it. They're some of the most famous and influential pieces to use when it comes to fighting evil spirits and demons. Although a secret document says that there is one ring that gives you the power of all 44, that's the one we're looking for Last seen was in your local museum before the storms hit your town. It's our only clue right now so we gotta look there tomorrow. Sleep if you have to. Imma go take a shower," She got up and went to the bathroom. I went off to my room and lay in my bed. What am I doing? What did I start? And What did Mae mean when she said a "certain someone"? I wanted to talk about this, but tonight I wanted to forget it. I know I'm going to ask about it tomorrow for sure. I turn over to sleep, and I see Yosuna in one of my sweats. "What are you doing?" I asked, "Sleeping here too, What else?" She answered. She had a blanket and pillow with her too. I would have told her to sleep on the couch, but the way she looked sent butterflies that tickled my whole body. "what?" She asked, "Nothing, it's fine, do what you want. Goodnight" I said turning to hide my bashful expression. "Alright then, Goodnight," she said. I thought she mistook my answer for no, and truthfully, I hope she didn't. But I felt her step on the bed, and I scooted over. She lay next to me facing the other way. I didn't know what to make of this, but I didn't want it to end. Is that wrong?

CHAPTER 6

The morning came something new had happened. For the first time in about 2 weeks, I didn't have the same nightmare. I was kinda relieved, I thought it wouldn't end. I went to get up, but I felt something holding me. Yosuna has turned around and had her arm wrapped around me. I got nervous instantly. I moseyed out of bed and went to the kitchen to make cereal. After I had sat down in the living room with my breakfast, I thought about the last two days and what's gonna happen today. In fact, I don't even know what we're doing today. All Yosuna said was we start tomorrow, but I don't even know what step one is. Wait, the items were called the Seal of Solomon, that means that Arashi was one who has the ring, so I just gotta find him. I heard a knock on the door. "who is it?" I asked walking up to my door. "Yo, It's me Arashi, I gotta tell you something about that ring I found yesterday." He said. Speak of the devil. I opened the door and let him in He had his backpack with him too. He started his story the moment he saw me: "Ok so after I left you to get the reward for the ring I found. I ran into a weird guy in a suit who pulled up in a limo. He told me he just left from there, brought up how he was looking for the lost items too. The thing is he wanted to buy them. He said he was a collector and offered twice as much as the museum did, he even had a business card. So I sold it. Long story short. I'm loaded sort of haha!" Shit, another dilemma that I have to deal with. I couldn't believe what I heard. until Arashi pulled out his backpack and emptied it. He wasn't kidding, there was nothing but cold hard cash falling out his bag. "50,000 dollars, I took 3 and a half hours to count it myself." He said with a smile like the kid who got the biggest bag of candy on Halloween. I didn't know what to even think about this. "What-what are you gonna do now?" I asked him because that's practically the only question yet. "That's why I'm here. I came to see if you wanted to spend some of it with me" He answered cheerfully "We could go to the amusement park, the mall, or I could just get a girl, and we could double date at the movies with you and your girl. Nice work by the way" He said finally pointing towards my room. Yosuna was standing there in my clothes.

"I knew you were lying about why you skipped class haha, I hope I didn't interrupt anything," Arashi said with a slight smile. That's the same thing Kenshi said, smile and all. "No, you didn't," I told him, being sure he heard it. "Oh so you got done haha, cool," Arashi replied without missing the point. "Gah- that's not what I meant!" I said quickly. He gets me with crap like that all the time. Although It's actually kinda funny. Yosuna didn't seem to care. "Cereal," was all she asked. Then I remembered. "But we do have something, we've got to do today so it might not be the best time," I told Arashi, I hadn't exactly lied, but it wasn't necessarily the truth. Hoping he wouldn't pry into why we gotta go. Arashi calmly replied "Hey, the first girl in you brought home. If you wanted more private time. Ya don't gotta hide. I get it," he doesn't get it, but that wasn't the case. Arashi then pulled out about 500 dollars and said: "here knock yourself out, treat her good I'm gonna head off to classes early," So that's how he does it. He gave me the money and refused to take it back. He put the rest of the money back into his backpack and started to head out the door. He turned around and called to Yosuna "Yo, be easy with him would ya. I'm leaving it up to you then," He's gone laughing "man-eh DUDE!" I stammered embarrassed. "At least your friends care for ya haha," Yosuna chuckled lightly. All bs aside, I got a new problem, I thought that the ring would at least be at the museum. So now, I gotta find out who Arashi sold the ring to. Looking at the money he left me, I noticed something. There was a small white slip, I picked it up, it was a business card with gold stripes and lettering. It had a phone number and address. The name read: "Dr. Alexander Mordecai. Surgeon, Psychologist, DDS" Damn, either he's lying, or he's practically everything. Then lastly, it read: "Private Collector," of course he is. "Whats that?" Yosuna asked while still eating, I guess asking her about table manners is pretty redundant. I explained what happened and showed her the card. "So your friend had the ring and sold it to this private collector? Hell, he might actually have some more useful stuff to help us too. Hey, I got an idea, let's go check and see if he has the ring when you come back." she said examining at the card. She's on point with a lot of stuff and far off on others, I don't think I'll get used to it. I Got what I needed and headed off to class. I didn't know what next, so I guess its a start.

I was just walking to school. I have no clue what think at this point. First, I learned that things that shouldn't exist, do exist. I almost died more times in the last three days than in the past three years. Last but not least, I can't even relax when I get home because I gotta figure out how the hell. Now I gotta help her fix this crap. At least I'll be able to sleep in a class or two today. I got to school and went through everything ok. I was walking out of the last morning class when Mae walked up to me, nope not again. The moment I turned to walk away. "Wait, I'm sorry," she said as she grabbed my hand: "I'm sorry about yesterday, it's just the rumors stated that you were cold, heartless, but I saw what a kind person you are. I shouldn't have done that to you. You had the chance to kill me, and you let me live," I can feel her honesty in her touch this time, so I stayed and accepted her apology. I also had some questions of my own to ask. "Hey, what did you mean when you said it takes a certain someone to break the seal?" I asked her. That question's been on my mind ever since she said it. "So Yosuna didn't tell you yet huh?" Mae responded with a question. "I never got around to asking her. Speaking of which, how do you know Yosuna anyway?" I asked. I was really hoping Mae would be the only one I'd ask. She pondered for a second, then she started to explain about what she said. : "You see, the thing is, not just anyone can release Lucifer and Hades. You have to be a being of their freakishly insane caliber, and honestly," she leaned in closer: "I believe it. When a vampire bites someone, their prey is supposed to be rendered paralyzed regardless of what. But when I bit you there was something that rejected me and gave you more strength. The only way to explain that is that there's more to you than anyone knows," I'm not sure how to feel about that. "How do you know Yosuna?" I asked her, "She's more famous than you think. I can't tell you anymore. You're gonna have to ask her about the rest, I mean she's your watchdog right. Gotta go. Bye," Mae said as we parted ways. On my way home. Walking back I started thinking I never really asked yosuna any questions. How does she know who I was, how did she know where to find me and what the fuck was she doing with that box anyways? I realized that I hadn't asked her about any of that. I need to have a talk with her when I get home. I don't know exactly what's going to happen from here, but I do not like being left in the dark.

I got home to find Yosuna was still wearing my clothes. She washed all of hers, and she's still wearing my clothes. "What are you doing?" I asked She seemed to be having something heating on the stove. "What does it look like? I'm making something to eat before," she answered. So she cooks too, another thing I didn't know about her. It looks delicious too, it was some kind of soup, but it had a very sweet smell to it. wait. First, I needed to ask her about everything before I get caught up in the pleasant atmosphere. "Hey can I ask you about something,": "Yeah, wassup," she replied. I asked her: "The two medallions. Why did you have them in the first place? What are you?". She stopped, wiped her hands on a towel and replied:."I was taking them to get put back into the cave's safe. After Lucifer and Hades had been sealed, the relics were supposed to be replaced back in the cave to lock and hide purgatory. But, the war was so great, the relics were lost and never rediscovered. Until 2 weeks ago. I was assigned to put them back and hide the realm. And to answer your other question, I'm a mercenary and so is your classmate." Of course, an answer leading to another problem. Apparently, one day she received an anonymous file with this as her objective. She said she was going to refuse then the lawyer paid her an extreme amount of money and told her she'll get the other half when the job is finished. But thanks to me, Lucifer and Hades are free, and we gotta start back at square one, which sounds pretty much impossible. Yosuna finished cooking and walked into the restroom. "I'm gonna get ready to head out, eat then come on," She said as she shut the door. The shit I do for people, really. We got ready and left to see the private collector from the business card Arashi dropped. We do know he has the ring, the only problem is how are we going to convince him to just let us borrow it? I don't have any idea where we go from here, but it seems like she's got a plan. Needless to say, square one is going to be problematic. "Oh and be careful, a lot of people wound up going missing while traveling through there" She finished. Son of a-

CHAPTER 7

We took off to the collector's house, but he didn't live close at all. We took a transit that lasted damn near 3 hours. I mean, the scenery of the countryside was amazing but damn. On the way there while looking at all the trees pass by I look at Yosuna. She has a focused look on her face, no matter how I see her, she's still cute. She had a backpack with her, it must be where she keeps her info on her mission. We got to his house and man this guy isn't shy about his wealth. There was a big gate with a new, cut, green yard and wilderness in the back. Yup, it's the country alright. Although he had an ordinary house. It looked more like a cabin, twice the size of a house, with the porch going all the way around. Stone chimney with a smell of firewood. At least he's humble. We see the front gate and a screen on the left pillar. I walk up to it to ring the bell. "Hold it," Yosuna said as she put her backpack down and began to search for something. "Uh...why?" I asked. "He's not home right now," she replied. She pulled out a 3 point grapple hook attached to a link line and loaded it in a pistol. "What are you doing with that?" I asked looking at the hook. She just smiled, winked and said: "making our way in," Aw, crap. As soon as she said that, she grabbed me, shot the hook over the wall and in a quick zip we flung over the gate. "Holy Crap!" I yelled out while we landed on the roof, rolling off into the bushes out back. Yosuna stood up and lit a cigarette, I know damn well it isn't tobacco either. "Whew that was fun, come on," She said. That wasn't a pleasant fall. My back hurts now. We had to sneak our way to the front door because he still had security cameras, we just wound up landing in the blind spot. "Why are we sneaking in, couldn't we just talk to him or something," I asked. She started picking the lock and replied: "if it were that easy, we wouldn't be doing this," Great, now we're breaking and entering. This is just getting better and better. After about a minute, there were two clicks and the door unlocked. "Got it," Yosuna said. Suddenly, a light alarm went off, then the floor disappeared

It was a trap door, and we fell right in. "AAAH!," I yelled as I slid down a hatch with Yosuna sliding in front of me. From the looks of it, she seemed like a kid in the park, "WOOHOO!" she yelled laughing. We fell down the tunnel into a solid white room with a glass door. What the hell? What kind of security system is this? I looked around, the room was practically sealed off. Whoever got in here wasn't getting out, that meant us too. About two hours went by. "Great" I sighed "how the hell is we going to get out of here," Yosuna examined the room like I did a second ago and saw a security camera in the top corner of the room above the door. I'm not sure, but I think she "I Got an idea," she said she opens her backpack again and starts digging. I'm actually concerned about what she's going to grab next. She grabs two mountain spikes. "What the hell are doing with those!?" I stammered. She used the spikes to climb the wall then she grabbed the camera and jumped down. As she landed the wires attached to the camera began to bust out the wall. The wires seemed to be connected to the lock on the door as well. Yosuna then gave the wires one good yank and pulled the lock out the wall. She picked the lock on inside the hole on the door, causing it to slide open. I was speechless. We managed to get out of there but wound up to be in what looks like an exhibit room the gallery was massive. The house didn't look this big from the outside. Nothing but old relics and items from the 18th century to the late 1940's, so this has to be the doctor's collection, It was actually pretty amazing. All this stuff must be worth a fortune, also remembering how much he paid Arashi for the ring. How much did he pay for these? "hey, what the hell did you get me into?" I asked Yosuna starting to realize how serious this really is. "Calm down, were close to finding the ring, let's just get it and go," she replied. Walking towards the jewelry display of the collection. "I wouldn't do that if I were you," a voice said to us. We turned around to see who was behind us. A figure stood in the doorway on the other side of the room. It was a man, and his face, the left half of his face is melted from chin to the burned black space where his eye should be "Well well well, I'm impressed, you escaped my burglar room and even made it in here. You are aware that breaking and entering is a crime?" The man spoke again. So I guess this is the owner of the house, the collector, Dr. Alexander Mordecai

"So I take it you're the owner of this joint huh? Yosuna sighed lighting another blunt. Really, now's not the time to smoke. "Yes, I am" Alexander calmly replied as he pulls a revolver and shoots the blunt from her hand. "And I would appreciate it if you don't smoke in my house." Holy hell, this escalated way too fast. "Now, explain why you are here," He said standing there with the gun still pointed to us, Alexander looked at me kind of weird. There were rings on his fingers, they all had a different sigil on each one. I look to Yosuna to see what to do now. She calmly put up her hands up as I did mine. Of course, at the last second as always, She grabbed me by the arm yelled: "RUN!" and hauled ass to the door on the other side of the room, dragging me with her. At this point were running from gunfire, an alarm sounded off, and we have no idea how to get out of the house we broke into. There was an open door that led to a hallway, Yosuna threw me in the door and shut it behind her, locking it. "WHAT THE HELL!! I barked at her. "Hey, now's not the time to bitch alright, go," She responded pushing me on ahead. It got quiet, so we started to go trough the hall. There seemed to be 5 doors on each side of the corridor numbered 1-10. It suddenly got cold, and the doors were different than the one on our cell. It was a steel door with a small square window with bars. What's worse, I think people might be locked in there. I managed to get a clear view of the locks. Talk about advanced. How did Yosuna crack that? Then there was a sudden, BOOM! "What was that?" I gasped, I checked the door next to me, door 8. It was a guy that looked around my age with messy black hair covering his face, he saw me "h-Hey! You! Let us out please!?," The guy stammered as he was breathing heavily. There was a brand of some sort with the number of the door on his chest. There was blood on his face, no, not just his face. There was blood everywhere, the walls of his room, on his torn clothes, the look in his eyes screamed crazy, and his teeth didn't look human at all. They were like animals, a beast of some kind. It was frightening. Wait, Us? does that mean there are more people locked in these rooms? "Takashi Come on," Yosuna called out to me. I backed away from the door and followed her out the hall. I could still hear the captive yelling: "HEY! COME BACK!! LET US OUT!! COME BACK!! Pounding on the door. BOOM, BOOM, BOOM!

We ended up in some operating room. This room is by far the creepiest thing yet. The room was dark, it was sealed together like a safe with only one light bulb over the operating table, and there's blood on that too. We went past that into an office. I felt more like I was in a hospital than a house. The room was filled with posters of sigils and ancient markings and it's a dead end. This quickly transitioned from home to an asylum. There were two windows, one looking into the operating room, another looking into what seems to be a giant battle cage this was not getting any BETTER!!. There was a control panel under the second window, must be connected to the two rooms. The desk was covered with an anatomy of different people. The on the top of the stack read:" It has been 56 months since I've started my research. Only a select few were barely able to survive the full input of power from my experiments. Not only that, I have successfully created the survivors into some of the most fascinating and compelling breeds of genetic hybrids the world has ever seen. I have yet to put them to battle against the monsters I've gathered from the other realms. The only objective now is to find a way to infuse their souls with the power of the seals in order to completely control them. If such method is possible I'll have the vengeance on Hades that I wanted. I have not yet figured out how to brand the five due to their healing factor sealing the wounds. I branded them with numbers before the experiments which appear to be the only scar remaining on each of the subjects. If possible I will find a way to infuse them with the sigils power, I will use it to create an army to bend to my will and have power rival to a demi-god." What kind of crap is this? Yosuna locked the office door and started to push random buttons on the control panel. I look through the window, and I can see the collector and his men trying to break down the door of the hallway. "What Are you doing?" I asked her. "Trying to see if one of these buttons could get us out of here," She answered just slamming buttons on the panel until she hit a button that sounded off an automated voice on an intercom "WARNING!! All holding cells have been unlocked, WARNING!! All holding cells have been unlocked" The voice played out. But we were still stuck. Yosuna grabbed me "TAKASHI, we gotta go." she yelled grabbing my arm. We ran out the office and through the operating room to find Alexander just broke down the door. He walks in with his revolver and a huge group of goblins and trolls. Please don't tell me this is his security. "what have you done?" Alexander said with an enraged look on his face as he raised his weapon. Then the doors in the holding cell hallway opened up, and one person walked out of five doors. Four guys, one girl, then dead silence

CHAPTER 8

Just one hallway, Yosuna and I on one side, The collector and his henchmen on the other, with the five captives from the holding cell in the middle of us. The prisoners all had the same brand each with a different number, #3, #6, #7, #9. In the midst of the five was #8 the prisoner I saw beating on the door. He still had that crazed look in his eyes looking back at them and us. "GET THEM!!" Yelled the collector, his henchmen charged towards us but was stopped. #8 had the goon by his throat. the goon fired his gun four times into #8 with every round I see the blood falling on the floor. The captive lets out a sudden growl, then in a quick motion pulled back his hand. My stomach jumped, forcing my voice to crack loudly: "OH SHIT!!". H-holy crap, the prisoner ripped out his throat!! There was blood, everywhere, you could hear the henchman gurgle while gasping for air. As he fell to the ground wasting his last breath, the other captives joined in. #6 looked directly at me, he winked at me and smiled. Then in a zip, he was gone. A green light flashed, I heard a sudden sound of bones cracking, then he was in front of me. The moment I saw him again, four more henchmen fell lifeless. My stomach dropped. What, what was that? Dead, they were dead, just like that. #3 was just throwing goons into each other like ragdolls. #7 and #9 both managed to get their hands on a couple of guns and started shooting the rest of the goons. I'm really going to die this time. The collector ran out of the room. Before I could comprehend anything else, it was just me, Yosuna and the 5 captives standing over a floor full of dead bodies. The five of them were staring at the two of us. Yosuna was focused, but I was sweating bullets. Then the five dropped their weapons, and #8 spoke: "Thank you," His wounds were all healed not a single trace indicating that he was shot and he looked healthy. only a few scars were there, along with the #8 branded on him. none of that came from what just happened. Another quiet zip sounded with a green streak, and #6 stood next to #8 "Nah, he's not kiddin' It's been so long I forgot the taste of pizza," said #6 laughing. #8 swung towards him, and #6 dodged it and zipped to the other side of #9. He's so fast. I haven't even blinked yet, and he disappeared twice already, running back and forth. "Despite him being an idiot, he's not exaggerating," said #9. "we have been locked up in here for months on end, almost years. so we really do appreciate you breaking us out of here." Then, another sound came from the other rooms, it seemed like more monsters were coming our way. "we must go now," said #8

"Now," #8 stated to #3 as both of them looked and simultaneously punched the wall. It was like dynamite, a great hole was blasted into the wall. The hole led into the room with the battle cage. As soon As we walked in the doors all around the chamber shut, and we're trapped. The only light on was in the ring. The collector's voice sounded from the intercom. He is in the office where the control panel was. "You!! for some simple burglars, you really picked the wrong house this time, and to you five. I knew I shouldn't have let you live, but I'm not angry. No, this is actually an opportunity to see the fruit of my labor. I want to run one final field test against the other monsters I've gathered and created from the other realms. Let us see if you can survive." The door under the window opened, and he had a monster of all kinds. It was a horrible sight. Some monsters looked like they were just put together with staples. They seemed more like stumbling, rotten, filthy corpses. But there was A LOT of them, and they can run, Damn they can RUN! #8 started running towards the beasts, and the other of the five weren't behind. the three-armed Cyclopes was the biggest one in the group and swung down a stone hammer that was bigger. #8 threw a left uppercut aiming at the hammer. He shattered the hammer-head crumbling it into pieces. He then followed with a right cross that literally popped the head off the creature. The other bigger monsters started charging. #3 hit a beast with a three-hit combo, ripped off its arm to use it like a baseball bat. #6 zipped off, all you could see was a light green streak passing by picking parts off, limb from limb. #7 grabbed the weapons and used them as projectiles, she did seem to miss either. Meanwhile, Yosuna and #9 was just fighting like hardcore assassins. I was making sure that I wouldn't get killed in the midst of everything. I analyzed the room to see if there was a way to get out. The collector is in the office that we used to break out the captives helping us, so that means we need to use that as a way to escape. I look to where the monsters are coming from, there seems to be a hatch leading underground. "HEY!!" I yelled pointing at the hatch, "DOWN THERE!!" I'm sure they heard me because #3 grabbed a monster and used it as a shield to make a pathway to the hatch. Holy hell, #3 is like a rhino. He was trampling his way through while we followed behind him.

So what's the point here? Oh, it's good to be curious, but if warnings tell you not to mess with something, DON'T mess it!! We had monsters of all kinds making sure we don't get to the door. "Ahh, what a bitch-Gah!!!" I heard #8 said as cyclopes twice his size jumped behind him, impaling him. #8 turned around, breaking the blade that stabbed him. At the same time, he hit the cyclops to the side and punched a hole in its chest. The beast fell as the man freakishly fought off others one by one, his wounds healing rapidly. One hitter quitters with every blow, his voice changed he says: "come on. That all ya got?" #9 was hitting them with everything and they just kept coming. "hey, come on people!" said #6 zipping by the hatch door, keeping a clear path. We managed to get passed and get everybody into the hatch. #8 attempted to close the door pushing up with all the monsters running towards the door. a cracking of bones sounded off, "Arggh," #8 grunted, holding the door, he might pack a mean punch, but he doesn't get that from his strength. #3 assisted and shut the door in one push, crushing whichever monsters' limbs were caught between the crack a light green streak seeped in before the door shut. "You suck!!, all that for a pack of cigarettes?" It was #6 he ran in the door at the last second. "C-mon, I knew you were going to make it," Said

#9 grabbing the pack of smokes from him. It was dark, but we were able to see. It looked like a cave, certainly a place to keep your monsters you can't fix. "We can find our way out through here," #8 said pointing to an opening. "Wait," Yosuna said keeping her grip on my hand. "Who are you guys, and why did that psychopath of a doctor have you in there for?" #8's voice changed again as he answered, "I can explain if while we find a way out, but we have to keep moving" I think I already know who they are and if I'm right, following them out would be a good idea.

As we followed the captives through the tunnels, #8 reminded us to keep watch. We still had a bit of a way to go, so we weren't out yet, "can we find a bar after this, I need a drink," said #9 lighting up a cigarette. #6 walked nest to him and asked: "this whole time we've been locked in there, all you're worried about is drinking?" #9 responded with a look that answered the question. #6 turned and shrugged his shoulders, "Nevermind," I'm still pondering over how this has been the longest and most stressful day of my life. At that split second, I remembered the paper I read on the desk in the office from earlier. "The experiments, you guys are the survivors, aren't you?" I asked to be sure. #6 zipped next to me." sweet, you believe crazy, that's a relief," he said. #7 responded: "Yes, we've been locked away for at least two or three years. In the beginning, there were over fifty of us, now as far as we know, we're what's left,". "It was referred to as the 100 experiment project, and we were the guinea pigs," said #8 bumming a cigarette from #9. #9 scoffs: "humph if you ask me, they just found 100 bullshit excuses to carve us up," "What's he mean by that?" Yosuna asked. "The many of us that were kidnaped weren't random, we were chosen. Supposedly we have blood relations to higher powered beings," #8 explained. "I'm sorry," I asked baffled. "Aww, don't stop believing now. This is the best part. Our parents are gods man or something like that," #6 butted in, he speaks awfully fast. Wait, hold up, GODS!?! come on man, I just want to go home. "unfortunately, we had to learn the hard way. well since we've gotten this far, might as well introduce ourselves, right?" #8 concluded by giving their names in number order from least to great, 3, 6, 7, 8, 9. So their names were Varo, Chris, Iri, Lawrence, and Dominic. We introduced ourselves as well. "We're not necessarily sure who our parents are, though, but I guess he already knew since that bastard just took us without question," Lawrence said puffing smoke. "What were yall doing here anyway?". "He released nearly every demon lord known to belief and possibly started the apocalypse," Yosuna answered casually pointing at me. Chris laughed "Holy crap dude that sucks," "There was an item that we needed to get from this house, and you can pretty much guess from there," Yosuna finished. "well, If you never showed up, we probably would've been still locked in there so I'm not complaining," Lawrence sincerely said with relief. "Hey guys, it opens over here. Let's go," Chris called out to us from ahead. Then a sudden crash busted a hole in the ceiling, and someone fell through. It was a monster and man it was a big one

CHAPTER 9

This was something that was frightening, The beast looked to be a minotaur and Cyclopes hybrid. It was massive in size, his horns were covered in blood, and he had one eye. "It's him, the monster who killed all the patients who tried to escape," Iri said setting in a fighting stance. Lawrence ran towards the beast throwing a right, the creature caught his hand, struggled and twisted his arm, breaking the bones out his skin. The ground rumbled. "AARGH!!!" Lawrence yelled as the beast head-butted him in the chest, throwing him back ten feet and putting two holes in his chest from the beast's horns. Chris and Dominic charged towards the beast fighting. The monster overpowered with sheer strength and force. The creature let out a roar and advanced until Iri Started shooting it with razor-edged shards she made out the stone tunnel walls. Varo engaged and matched the monster in strength, they were at a stalemate trying to overpower one another. Varo landed two hard ones in the face and thrown the beast onto the ground. Then all at once, the four demi-humans started to attack the beast, dropping it to its knees. I also heard a slow sound of bones cracking. I turned to see Lawrence standing there with the holes sealed shut. He walked to the beast crackling and straightening his arm, balling his hand to fight. The others moved back as Lawrence, and the oversized experiment went at it. After a moment of exchanging blows, the creature lets out a growl and attempted to break the same arm a second time, it didn't work. Lawrence let out a more devastating noise, reversed the attack and completely twisted the monster's arm in a way it shouldn't turn, then grabbed the other arm and did the same. You can hear the beast roar in pain. The Cyclopes-minotaur was down to a knee unable to move its arms. Lawrence cranked his right arm and landed a solid blow to practically cripple the thing as he cracked both his hand and started to work on the head like a punching bag. He just kept hitting blow after blow, right and left, going faster with every punch. Knocking the monster's head in. I saw the expression he had along with tears. His eyes were glowing yellow, they have focused anger, pure rage knowing where to be applied. "That's enough, he's down," I yelled trying to step in, but Dominic stepped in front of me, and Chris zipped next to him. I wasn't going to get through them. I then realized that it wasn't just Lawrence, all five of them had a different glow but the same fire in their eyes. In one final move, Lawrence gripped the monster by the top of the head, pulled as hard as he can, decapitating it by force. "Humph, I guess you can't break a minotaur's horn, You son of a bitch!" Lawrence uttered just holding the head as blood is splashing around. I may not know what exactly is going on, but I don't think I wanted to either. All you heard was a thud of a lifeless body falling to the floor.

Lawrence stood there panting, for a second before he faced us. His eyes had completely changed, they lightly glowed yellow with diamond-shaped pupils. I just couldn't comprehend anything anymore. Also, it seems like this time even Yosuna had no clue what to make of this. His eyes started to fade back to normal. Without saying anything, he walked ahead leaving the remains of whatever the hell that was. We managed to escape out of the tunnels, I look back and we were also outside the gate of the property as well. we ran into the wood. Just exactly what the hell was that? At first, they were fighting to get out of confinement but that last one. That was brutality brought overboard. I was rendered silent for a minute. Yosuna asked if I was okay. "I'm sorry you had to see that," Lawrence said "but if you knew half of the things it has done to us, you would feel the same way," Then an unpleasant voice spoke to us. "Wonderful, I love it. The rage, the relentless violence, looks like my hypothesis turned into fact," It was the collector. "You seem doing well, keeping in mind that you have the most potent healing factor. as for the rest of you, despite not using your full potential, you all showed much promise with your progress," Lawrence charged at Alexander but was Spartan kicked back with a force. The others charge in but were stopped by the same force. Even Chris, who was like the flash or something, was caught by his neck. The collector gave Chris a solid knee then kicked him back. Varo and Dominic attacked simultaneously but were outmatched. The collector grabbed Varo, slammed him onto the ceiling and the ground then threw him into Dominic, Chris, and Iri like a bowling ball. Yosuna tried to fight too and kept up a bit before he roundhouse her. Lawrence engaged again. Alexander grabbed Lawrence by his arm and started choking him. Lawrence threw punch after punch with a solid right to the jaw, it connected but had no effect. Smiling, Alexander said: Here's the thing, you may heal fast," He punched Lawrence so hard in the gut, blood spilled. "But you're not unstoppable," with that said, the collector began landing blow after blow, to the gut, then to the face, knocking Lawrence out. I tried to step in then the collector pointed towards me with an awful satisfied expression. "You, stay put Mr. Azuno, Yes I know who you are,"

Everyone was knocked out while the doctor spoke: "I've studied your name. for quite a while until now I didn't know what you looked like, then you just so happen to be the one who broke into my home. I also know how to help you with your little problem about Lucifer and Hades,"; "What," I asked, how does he know this much about me? "Yes, you play a much bigger role in all of this than you seem to perceive. Well as you may know from going into my research, I am a man who believes in the world of the supernatural. I am also a man who is...bored with this world but yet still had some unfinished business here also. When news came to me first when I heard that hades were released from imprisonment and that instantly grabbed my attention. Like you Mr. Azuno, I'm just someone preparing for such events but not for shelter, for battle." His voice was calm, cold, even convincing. "You see, I have a bit of a personal vendetta against the God of the Underworld. He is the reason I look this way, why my perfect life was...

Ruined. You're the one I need to complete my project, so you sir are going to help me with my research." This guy can't be serious. Before anymore was said, a green streak zipped by the collector three times, hitting him. the streak hit him one more time backward into the tunnel. It was Chris, seems he had already gotten the rest of the group outside. "GO NOW!!" The walls were shaking, they were caving in. Chris grabbed me and before I could even blink, my stomach turned upside down while I was standing with the others outside. I wanted to know what was that about but I didn't want to ask. I also remembered, at that moment, the whole reason why we were even here. "Wait, the ring. We didn't get the freaking ring." I starting to complain about almost dying for something I didn't get. Yosuna tapped my shoulder. "actually," She said holding up the ring smiling. I was overjoyed I just hugged her without thinking even once. "HA, I KNEW IT!" Chris yelled nudging Lawrence "You owe me a bag," Lawrence just smiled and even chuckled as he said: "yeah, yeah, whatever man. Takashi, Yosuna, since you got us out of there we owe you one" "Uhh....Guys" Varo said, "You might want to see this unless you have a weak stomach," We walked next to him to see what he saw. There were animals, slaughtered, just parts everywhere. It was gruesome with a smell so foul I couldn't help but to puke. "What the hell happened here?" Dominic asked. The blood on the ground made the same marks and signs that were on the sigils in the office room. "It's a ritual," Yosuna answered, "It's starting, every big evil being within mythology is trying to recreate the apocalyptic war." "I'm sorry did you say war?" Iri asked Chris looked a bit more upset than the rest of the group pouted and said "So much for opening a cock-fighting ring,"

Yosuna examined the area a little bit more, "It's okay," she said, "from the looks of it, it was a communication ritual," She then picked something up from the ground. It was a sheet of paper folded into four. "it's a note, seem like the doctor was trying to call somebody" she said opening and reading the page. "It's a journal page, seems that everybody knows about you Takashi, except for about what you look like. and everyone is on board with trying to get everything back to normal, except for one catch," I felt uneasy when she said that. "there's another way to fix everything it's just, the one who released them must be sacrificed to do it," son of a BITCH!! "what!?!," I asked "In order to fix everything, they need to kill you,. Lucky for us, we're a couple steps ahead. so, for now, let's go back and rest." Yosuna answered as she sighed. Just perfect, at least we get some kind of comfort. Still, the fact that now people are going to be after me, my life is going to suck. We wandered until we found the road leading into the town Yosuna and I arrived at when we came out here. We stopped by the local shop where Chris zipped in and out, getting everyone a new change of clothes. Dominic hit him upside the head for getting him a girl shirt the first time as a joke. We took the same three-hour transit back to my place and I'm not sure why but everybody followed me home. "Why are you guys here?" I asked "Hell, we ain't got anywhere to go," Chris replied without missing a beat. "How the hell am I going to have five people living in all in my place, are you insane?" I asked. "No no no, not like that," Dominic assured him "Hey! The new tenants are here! and you showed them how to get here, nice Takashi" what?

I turned to see Kenshi smiling. Chris walks up to Kenshi and hands him some money. "Here's first-month rent," He said. I was completely baffled. well, I still have the place to myself. "Oh and Takashi, I'm sure your lady friend has already told you, but I approved her to stay with you at your apartment," Kenshi said to me. Say what now? I looked to Yosuna and she just smiles and winked like she always does. Okay so after a very, VERY, long day of complete chaos, the girl linked to all of it has to LIVE with me now? Yosuna hugged me from the back, saying "Yup, we're all set," She was giving me major butterflies and fuzzy feeling. Well, I guess it isn't all bad. Later, after we got inside the apartment and set our stuff down, I took a shower and went to bed. Again, Yosuna came to my room to share my bed because She doesn't have one yet and refuses to sleep on the floor. I really didn't mind at all. Hell, I started to catch myself counting on it now. The butterflies, nor the fuzzy feeling never stopped as I drifted off to sleep.

CHAPTER 10

I went to sleep and drifted off into another dream but this one was different. "That's because this time it isn't just a dream," said a voice in my head that isn't mine. Someone tapped my shoulder. I turned to see Yosuna. Now I'm not sure if I heard that right. "Say what now, what are you talking about, what's happening now?" I asked, not really sure what she's talking about? I rose up looked around to see that I was floating above my bed, and in it, I saw myself laying asleep. I was speechless. What-what the hell is this? Yosuna calmly says: "Okay, don't freak out, it's all cool," could've fooled me. "What do you mean don't freak out!?" I barked. "Am, am I dead? Yosuna glared at me and said: "No, you idiot, this is lucid dreaming," what? "Everyone has it, but very little know how to use it or even tap into it, It's a way for the soul to leave the body and enter the spiritual realms, or the closest way of being dead without dying. since you actually went to purgatory, you managed to open the connection to that ability, which made it easier for me to access your mind through this." aw man, it's just one thing after another. the spiritual realm huh? "So what does this have to do with anything?" I asked. Yosuna calmly responded: "I'm going to show you the other realms that you don't know about, the ones connected through purgatory, see for yourself" She put her hand on my chest and pushed me into a hole in my wall. as I fell through I was somewhere else. an old village, like renaissance old. People were on horses, The road was dirt and not a single power line in sight. "You're in another realm. an alternate world where another mythology is existent as to yours. in your world, Christianity exists, greek mythology in another and so on," She grabbed me and started to fly across the realm. I was somewhere else, families were outside enjoying almost every aspect of life. kids were playing, the neighbors were all smiling and I can feel the sincerity in their smiles. I gotta admit, it was pretty amazing. seeing a new place where everything looked more peaceful than anything technology can offer. Then in an instant, the sky went red, a fire blazed in the background, a war was happening. It was horrible, appalling, I didn't want to see. The villagers were caught in the crossfire of the battle and were slaughtered. "This is a possibility of what might happen to your world," Yosuna said

"This, happened yesterday, that village was left in ruin with only very few survivors who've had to relocate to another realm. Not everything was restored. In the last war. about 19 entire realms were completely destroyed. "She brought me back to my bedroom. I was angry "Why are you showing me this- as a matter of fact why is this even happening to me? is it too much just to ask for a normal life? instead, I get this god knows what of a roller coaster!!," before I could say anything else, Yosuna quickly shoved me against the wall. "You need to quit being so goddamn selfish already!!, this whole time all you did was complain about was how your life isn't picture perfect and how you just got dragged into all this. Newsflash, as far as I'm concerned, you've been dealt a better hand than most people. You can actually change your hand, open your mind and don't waste this chance "There was a tear in her eye. She's right. I thought about Lawrence and the others. I was being a student in school while they were test subjects in someone's basement. "Takashi, if you don't stop this you won't have any chance at a normal life at all. We need you, I need you," She grabbed my hand and looked into my eyes like back then I can feel the sincerity in her words. My stomach piled up with so many butterflies. Then the sun started to shine through my window. "It's time to return to our bodies, "You will be rested when you wake up," Yosuna said She pushed me back to my body as a force pulled me in at the same time. All of a sudden black. as if I was just having another dream.

The next day finally came, I thought is never would. I got up and went to the kitchen to find Chris, Dominic, Lawrence, Iri, and Varo all in my apartment. "WHAT THE HELL!?!" I barked. "Shh, dude it's too early for noise, and don't worry we bought the food," Chris said, making coffee. "It's okay, I let them in," It was Kenshi, again. Despite that, I still have to do the dishes. Yosuna yawned walking up next to me "Whats going on?" she asked. "My kitchen is getting ransacked," I answered The group turned toward us "And there's the happy couple now, was last night fun? Oh, since

Yosuna told us about what your plan is we thought we'd help you. after all, stopping every apocalypse in belief isn't easy right "Lawrence chuckled. great, well I got some help now, that's cool. "Yeah, and the next step is to seal away Lucifer and Hades before someone gets the idea to introduce the rest of gang. Hell, they might actually be released right now so when you get back we have to get ready," Yosuna as we got dressed then sat down to have breakfast. It was actually nice to not have a quiet boring morning again. We had nice little conversations about what they used to be before the collector kidnapped them. Lawrence was traveling to be an aspiring writer. Dominic was a culinary master at a shop with major OCD about his work. Chris was a kleptomaniac who stole Lawrence's wallet, causing them to run into Dominic. Long story short, The were caught at the same time while fighting each other. Varo was on a path to bring peace among war and Iri made a living as an archery champion as well as knife-throwing. Seems like they all had a real set life before all this, It does make me happy to see them smile after hearing their stories, that's enough for me. I look at the clock to see I'm late to school again. "Aw, crap I gotta go," I said grabbing my backpack and ran out the door. Walking to school, I was thinking about What to do next. I have the ring that will help me win but something tells me there's more than that. My question was what kept these realms intact this whole time, I mean before I- Ah HEY!! What's going on here? Someone put a black bag over my head. I'm struggling to escape until a solid blow struck my crown, *WHACK, WACK* after the second strike. My conscious faded.